GW00367493

PINK
IS FOR GIRLS

WITHDRAWN
FOR SALE

sweatdrop
ORIGINAL UK MANGA STUDIOS
www.sweatdrop.com

200695736

WEST SUSSEX LIBRARY SERVICE	
20	0695736
LEON ·	17/7/09
WS 04/17	

PINK
IS FOR GIRLS

editor / Selina Dean
assisted by / Hayden Scott-Baron
cover design / Hayden Scott-Baron
cover image / Emma Vieceli
rear cover image / Sonia Leong

comics contributed by /
Emma Vieceli
Carrie Dean
Sonia Leong
Morag Lewis
Jacqueline Kwong
Aleister Kelman
Rebecca Burgess
Wing Yun Man
Niki Hunter

with additional writing by /
Mary Beaird
Fehed Said
Selina Dean

assistance and retouch by /
Ken Hoang
Morag Lewis
Selina Dean

All works © 2005 their respective authors. All rights reserved. No portion of this book may be reproduced or transmitted in any form or by any means without permission from the copyright holders.

Published by Sweatdrop Studios
www.sweatdrop.com

ISBN 978-1-905038-07-7

Printed in the UK
First printing, October 2006

foreword

By Helen McCarthy

400 words, they said. Something about "the nature of female sensibilities..." How would I know enough to write about the nature of female sensibilities? OK, I'm female, but I'd rather reason from the general to the particular; taking it outward implies that the world is made in my image, and last time I checked they lock you up for thinking you're God.

I like good writing and good art. I don't care if a male, a female or another species produces it, though I accept that I might have trouble understanding another species. Thereby, I think, hangs the myth of the female sensibility. Some people find life simpler if the world is divided in two, a pink sector for those who like hearts and flowers and a blue sector for those who prefer fast cars and casual violence.

The trouble is, people don't work like that. So there's a designated category of girly stuff, like makeup and fishnet stockings, forbidden to half the human race? Tell that to Eddie Izzard. Are women all pink and sugary and delicate? Tell that to Tracey Emin. Are men all big and macho and insensitive? Tell that to Stephen Fry. Does the fact that Johnny Depp was born to be drizzled with melting chocolate make him less or more of a man? (Pause for wholly gratituous sexual fantasy...) Girls can rave over Frank Miller or GTO, and men can go for Fushigi Yugi or Wendy Pini, without compromising their sexuality or their humanity. Men read women's writing; women read men's; artists draw for both sexes.

Men and women have differences, but so do Japanese and Americans, Christians and Buddhists, over-60s and teenagers. Gender isn't a dead issue by any means; not when women are still being circumcised before they're old enough to menstruate, sold into slavery before they're old enough to go to school, left to look after AIDS orphans when they're past retirement, forced to hold up half the sky with nothing more than hard work and endurance. But I honestly don't believe there are gender issues in Western commercial art. If you're good enough, your work will create its own audience.

So don't read this book because you think it's suitable for girls. Read it because you want to know what it's got to say. Don't let your chromosomes dictate your options – turn the page and get going.

Helen McCarthy has been around for a long time - she was watching anime before most of you were born, started researching it before the Internet went public and has been writing about it for two decades. She organised the UK's first convention anime programme and regular anime fanzine in 1990, edited the now-legendary (i.e. defunct) Anime UK magazine and the equally defunct Manga Mania, and wrote the first book in English on anime in 1993.

All this, and her short stature, might tempt those who place little value on their lives to call her the Yoda of anime. Please don't. Instead, buy the second edition of The Anime Encyclopedia when it comes out in November 2006. It's co-authored by Jonathan Clements.

preface

When we were coming up with the concept for this book, and its partner volume, *'Blue is for Boys'*, we couldn't have predicted how much hard work would be required. Not just the editorial work to put together two books at once, but from everyone, producing comics to fill what is, when combined as a pair, the largest Sweatdrop anthology yet.

The idea was too interesting to not follow through: to create two books, one for boys and one for girls, which while closely intertwined, explore the differences between shonen and shojo manga. In manga the differences between the genders runs deeper than simply tastes in genre – as girls sit down to read science fiction comics and boys buy volume upon volume of romance comics. Traditionally, one would expect it to be the other way around; certainly in this country people are brought up to believe that girls should be reading about ponies and kittens, and boys should be reading comics about the antics of delinquents. Yet in manga, we find every taste catered for, whether you're a boy or girl doesn't limit the type of story you can read.

Though the content found in manga transcends stereotypes, there are certain innate qualities and differences between manga for boys and manga for girls. Whether it's the literal verses the metaphorical, speedlines verses sparkles, or just a different perspective, shonen manga is distinctly boyish and shojo is distinctly girlish. In this volume, you will find nine stories for girls, each of which has a companion story in *'Blue is for Boys'*. The comics can be enjoyed alone, or with their partnered story.

We hope you like our book, whether you are a boy or a girl!

contents

9

10

......I WANT TO TELL HER

OF COURSE YOU DO!...

...JUST DON'T LEAVE IT TOO LONG!

SEE YA!

......

NOK NOK

CASS'...

NATASHA? WHY ARE YOU HERE?

!

I'M SORRY, TRISTAN BUT I COULDN'T LEAVE IT THERE...

CASS' WILL BE HERE ANY MOMENT!

I KNOW THAT! IT'S JUST ....

YOU HAVE TO TELL HER, TRISTAN!

I KNOW! I'M TRYING TO WORK UP TO IT....

I KNOW

BUT YOU HAVE TO TELL HER BEFORE SHE FINDS OUT FOR HERSELF....

BUT IT'S NOT EASY, NATASHA.

15

16

STORY AND ART
BY CARRIE DEAN

YAY! VOLUME 34 OF TWO HALVES WAS THE BEST SO FAR! THAT SCENE WITH THE FAT OLD PIRATE... HEEHEE

FRIENDS

ISN'T TWO HALVES COOL!!!

I LOVE TWO HALVES. PIRATES ARE AWESOME!

SIGH...

NO ONE SHARES MY PASSION.

SUCH PASSION
.....
I SPEND HOURS ONLINE OBSESSING

SPENDING ALL MY MONEY ON COLLECTABLES

SLEEPING WITH PLUSHIES

AND LOOKING AT ART.

FAP FAP FAP

HEY THERE, YOU WANNA BE A MEMBER OF MY CREW?

YES!

NOT INTERESTED.

REMOVE HER!

I DON'T CARE IF IT TAKES ALL THE BLOOD AND MONEY IN THE WORLD, I WILL BE A PIRATE ON THAT SHIP!

AND NO ONE CAN STOP ME!!!

25

Return to Chenezzar

By Sonia Leong

UGH...

ARE YE AWAKE?

WHO...

WHA... WHERE AM I?

FORGIVE ME, MI' LORD BUT...

I HAD FOUND YER LORDSHIP ON TH' ROAD...

...THA' LEADS TO CHENEZZAR

HAVING BEATEN THOSE DARK JESTERS SOUNDLY!

THERE'S
SOMETHING
ABOUT HER...

37

41

47

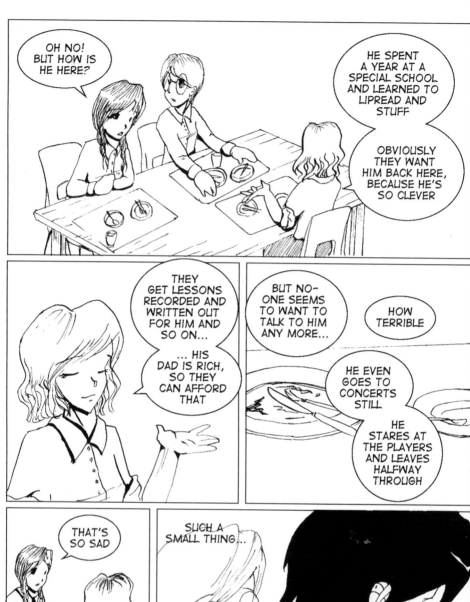

50

51

52

53

HE'S SO GOOD...

EVERY NOTE JUST AS IT SHOULD BE

VERY PRECISE, BUT...

THERE'S NOT MUCH FEELING IN IT

AH...

THAT'S BETTER

57

58

59

I WOULD LOVE TO COME

ANGEL'S GAME
Other Wings

Story by Mary Beaird

Artwork by Jacqueline Kwong

Edited by Ken Hoang

HAMALIEL, ROOK TO QUEEN'S BISHOP ONE.

[King to Queen's Bishop five]

BISHOP TO KING'S ROOK THREE, CHECKMATE. THAT WAS A PLEASANT GAME. PLEASE RESET

ISN'T IT FINISHED YET?

creak

I CANNOT SAY. IT WILL BE FINISHED WHEN IT IS FINISHED.

I'M BORED.

WE ARE NOT HERE TO BE ENTERTAINED, ALEXANDER.

REMIND ME, ESTELLE. WHY ARE WE HERE?

AH. YOU TEST ME. I HAVE NOT FORGOTTEN.

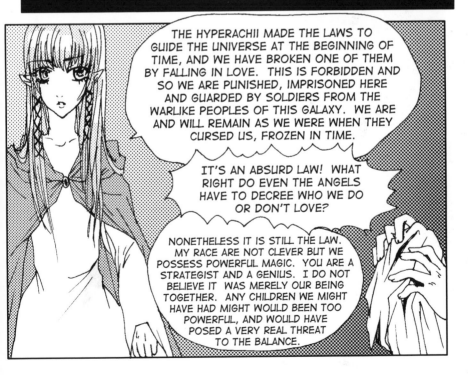

THE HYPERACHII MADE THE LAWS TO GUIDE THE UNIVERSE AT THE BEGINNING OF TIME, AND WE HAVE BROKEN ONE OF THEM BY FALLING IN LOVE. THIS IS FORBIDDEN AND SO WE ARE PUNISHED, IMPRISONED HERE AND GUARDED BY SOLDIERS FROM THE WARLIKE PEOPLES OF THIS GALAXY. WE ARE AND WILL REMAIN AS WE WERE WHEN THEY CURSED US, FROZEN IN TIME.

IT'S AN ABSURD LAW! WHAT RIGHT DO EVEN THE ANGELS HAVE TO DECREE WHO WE DO OR DON'T LOVE?

NONETHELESS IT IS STILL THE LAW. MY RACE ARE NOT CLEVER BUT WE POSSESS POWERFUL MAGIC. YOU ARE A STRATEGIST AND A GENIUS. I DO NOT BELIEVE IT WAS MERELY OUR BEING TOGETHER. ANY CHILDREN WE MIGHT HAVE HAD MIGHT WOULD BEEN TOO POWERFUL, AND WOULD HAVE POSED A VERY REAL THREAT TO THE BALANCE.

BUT WE PROMISED THEM WE WOULD NEVER HAVE CHILDREN. I WAS SATISFIED AND HAPPY JUST TO BE WITH YOU. I HAVE NEVER UNDERSTOOD WHY THEY COULDN'T SIMPLY LET US BE.

IT IS STILL IRRELEVANT. YOU THEY COULD TRUST, BUT I? MY PEOPLE ARE RULED BY OUR EMOTIONS. I WOULD HAVE BEEN TEMPTED, AND I WOULD HAVE BROKEN OUR VOW, SOONER OR LATER.

AND SO IT HAS BEEN AND WILL BE UNTIL THE TIME FORSEEN WHEN OUR MESSIAH WILL COME TO SAVE US...

..MY CURSE AND MY LOVE.

YOUR LOVE? YOUR LOVE? HOW DARE YOU CALL ME THAT NOW? WE HAVEN'T LOVED EACH OTHER FOR CENTURIES!

● ● ●

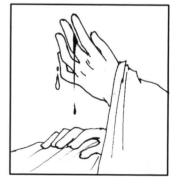

WHAT IS IT? ARE YOU HAVING...?

YES... A VISION.

THEN PLEASE, TELL ME.

Someone.. ...is coming

HAMALIEL! GIVE ME SCREENS. NOW!

HOLOGRAPHIC
PROJECTORS
SHUT OFF

DO YOU SUPPOSE
THAT THIS MAY
FINALLY BE THE
ONE?

I DON'T
KNOW

BUT THERE
HAVE ALREADY BEEN
SO MANY WHO HAVE
TRIED AND FAILED,
AND EVEN IF HE REACHES
US, IF HE GETS IT
WRONG, THE RISK...

YES. THE RISK
TO US ALL. I KNOW IT
ALL TOO WELL.
HAMALIEL? PLEASE OPEN
COMMUNICATIONS
WITH THE INTRUDER.

NOT PERMITTED. PUNISHMENT DICTATES THAT PRISONERS MAY NOT COMMUNICATE OUTSIDE THEIR DESIGNATED AREA.

PERMITTED FOR SECURITY PROTOCOLS.

GOOD. THEN CONTACT HIM. HELP HIM. GUIDE HIM TO US.

DAMN YOU HAMALIEL, I DON'T HAVE TIME TO ARGUE! ALOUD. IS CONTACT BETWEEN THE STATION COMPUTER AND THE INTRUDER PERMITTED?

AUTHORISATION?

NEGATIVE. ACCESS LOGIC. ASSESS INTRUDER PROGRESS THIS FAR AND CALCULATE ESTIMATED TIMES OF ARRIVAL BOTH WITH AND WITHOUT STATION COMPUTER INTERVENTION.

ESTIMATED TIME TO ARRIVAL WITH STATION COMPUTER INTERVENTION WOULD BE 15 MINUTES STANDARD. TIME WITHOUT INTERVENTION 38 MINUTES.

SO NOT TO COMPLY WOULD MERELY DELAY THE INEVITABLE OUTCOME. LOGIC?

LOGIC AFFIRMED

SO IN OTHER WORDS, WHAT DIFFERENCE DOES IT MAKE IN THE END?

PRECISELY. COME ON. I HAVE AN IDEA.

NOW!
YOU'VE GOT TO
DO IT NOW!

YOU MUST!

I CANNOT!
IT IS STILL
NOT TIME!

KRSSSHHHH

AHH!

STILL LOVE
YOU, LITTLE
MORTAL.

FORGIVE
ME, I WAS LYING
BEFORE. I STILL
LOVE YOU TOO.

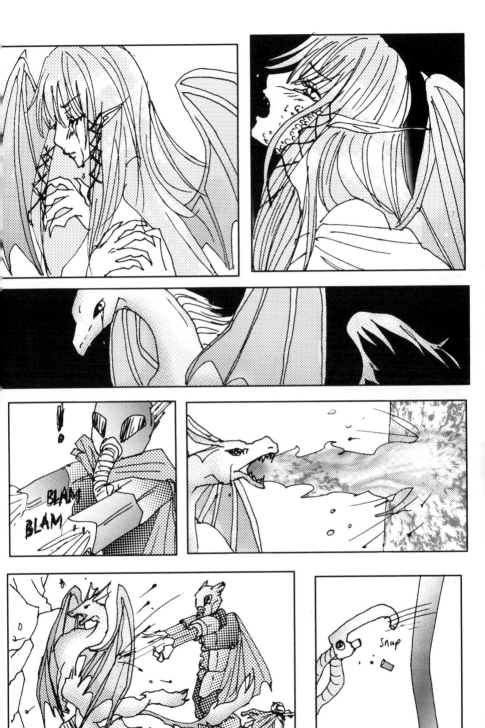

Brewing

story & art by **Aleister Kelman**

75

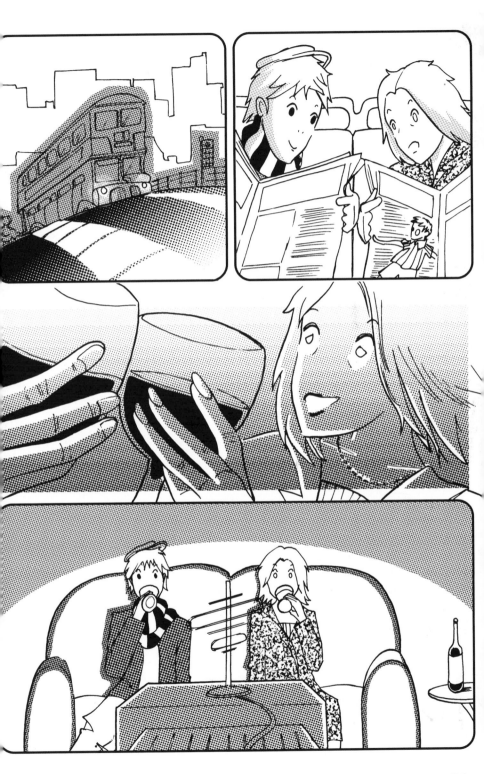

fin.

Hushed Notes

artwork by: Rebecca Burgess, **story by:** Fehed Said
inks by: Morag Lewis

91

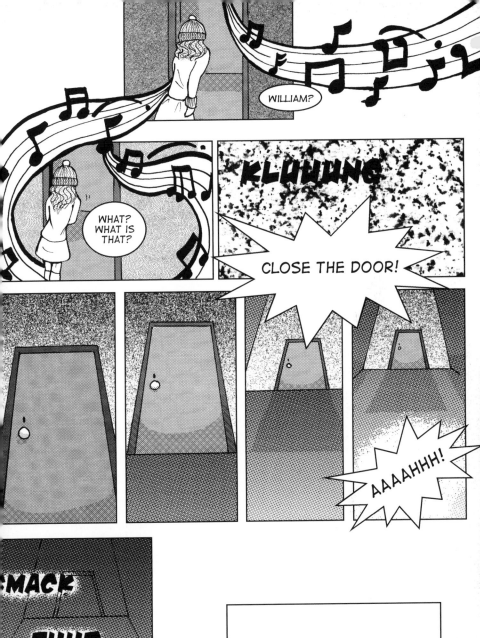

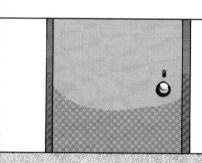

THE OLDER WE GET, THE WISER
WE ARE MEANT TO BECOME.
BUT WE NEVER CHANGE.

MAYBE SOME OF US
ARE DESTINED TO RELIVE
OUR MISTAKES.

MAYBE SOME OF US ARE
JUST BORN DAMAGED.

Magical Girl

Art: Wing Yun Man
Story: Selina Dean

MISS...

THAT GUITAR IS COMPLETELY AGAINST UNIFORM POLICY.

NOT TO MENTION THAT EARRING AND THAT SHIRT.

ARE YOU EVEN LISTENING?

NO.

YOU'LL MAKE ME LATE FOR MY GUITAR LESSON!

MY NAME IS MITSUKO.

I'M 15 YEARS OLD.

A LOT OF PEOPLE DON'T UNDERSTAND MY OBSESSION WITH PLAYING GUITAR.

OR WHY MY GUITAR ONLY NEEDS ONE STRING.

THE OTHER STRINGS BROKE LONG AGO...

BUT I DON'T BOTHER REPLACING THEM.

BECAUSE WHEN I STRIKE THIS STRING...

Metamorphosis

Story by Selina Dean
Art by Niki Hunter

ALL MY LIFE I'VE WANTED TO BECOME A BEAUTIFUL BUTTERFLY...

...BUT ALL I AM IS AN UGLY MOTH.

about us

Emma Vieceli
http://emma.sweatdrop.com
emma.vieceli@gmail.com
Emma Vieceli is the creator of *'Dragon Heir'* and an admin member of Sweatdrop. She is happy to see *'Give me my Romeo'* in this, Sweatdrop's latest anthology. She also provided the front cover artwork. Recent achievements include: being a winner of Tokyopop's Rising Stars of Manga, a winner of the Neo Magazine manga competition and earning a graphic novel contract adapting Shakespeare's Hamlet.

Carrie Dean
http://www.spanki.net
Carrie Dean enjoys illustration and design with an emphasis on cute! She is currently working on a comic, *'Kaia'*, and this is her first anthology piece. She hopes her story, *'Two Halves: Pink Skies'*, will bring a smile to your faces. She's just disappointed she couldn't get a gothic lolita girl in there. She should have tried harder!

Sonia Leong
http://www.fyredrake.net
sonia@fyredrake.net
Sonia is a core member of Sweatdrop and creator of *'Once Upon a Time'* and *'Cyborg Butterfly'*. Her contribution was *'Return to Chenezzar'* and the back cover art. Other achievements include Winner - NEO Magazine's 2005 manga competition; Judge - International Manga & Anime Festival; 2nd Place - Tokyopop's first UK Rising Stars of Manga competition. Her work appears in the British movie Popcorn (2006). Her manga adaptation of Romeo & Juliet will be published January 2007.

Morag Lewis

http://www.toothycat.net

Morag has been with Sweatdrop for three years, and is responsible for *'Looking for the Sun'* and *'Artifaxis'*, among other things. She wrote and drew *'Unheard Harmony'*. Apart from drawing and telling stories, she enjoys Tae Kwon-do, watching anime, reading and playing games, but is finding that, slowly but surely, the comics are taking over her life.

Jacqueline Kwong

http://lainnocence.deviantart.com

Jacqueline Kwong (a.k.a. Marbles) is the line artist for *'Angel's Game: Other Wings'* which was a collaboration project written by Mary Beaird and toned by Ken Hoang (a.k.a. Cin). Other works by Marbles under Sweatdrop are *'Dollhouse'* and *'Killer Cake'*. If you like her works please take the time to stop by her gallery at her website.

Aleister Kelman

http://www.ricecream.net

Aleister Kelman (a.k.a Keds) is an Illustrator and Graphic Designer working in London who finds it almost impossible to prevent Japanese style infiltrating his work. He is published in three of the four previous Sweatdrop anthologies and has his own book of short stories *'Falling Short'*. He plans to continue drawing and working for Sweatdrop until he eventually kicks the bucket.

Rebecca Burgess
http://bex.elvenblade.co.uk/
Rebecca Burgess is a budding artist and illustrator studying at art college. She has made several comics for Sweatdrop Studios, including a range of short stories, and her 6 part series, *'Illusional Beauty'*. Rebecca also has a webcomic adaptation of the opera, *'The Magic Flute'*, which can be found on her website.

Wing Yun Man
http://ciel-art.com
wing@ciel-art.com
Wing Yun Man is a freelance Illustrator and Character Designer who produced artwork for the mahou shoujo parody story *'Magical Girl'*. Her work has been featured in various media including books, magazines, corporate websites, events and more. Along with these appearances, Wing was also winner of the first 'International Manga & Anime Festival' competition held in 2004, for the 'Best Storyboard for Kids Category' as a major achievement.

Niki Hunter
http://www.vk-uk.com
visual.kei.in.the.uk@gmail.com
Niki Hunter is a full-time freelance artist with many years of experience in a range of creative fields, including the video games industry. In between freelancing, Niki has been developing her pet project *'VK-UK (Visual Kei in the UK)'*; including an exclusive VK-UK short comic featured in Sweatdrop's Sugardrops anthology. Niki hopes you will enjoy *'Metamorphosis'*, her second anthology piece for Sweatdrop.

Fehed Said

http://www.sixkillerbunnies.com

Fehed Said is proud to have been part of this exciting project and has had stories featured in Sweatdrop anthologies in the past. Other Sweatdrop works are *'co_OKiE'*, *'Faded & Torn'* and *'The Politics of Tears'*, with artwork by Shari Chankhamma, Keds and Emma Vieceli respectively. Recent titles by Fehed (with artwork from Shari) to have been picked up are the upcoming *'The Clarence Principle'* from Slave Labor Graphics and *'The Healing'* featured in the *'The Mammoth Book of Best New Manga'*. Fehed has some exciting Sweatdrop titles lined up for 2007. Keep an eye out.

YOU'VE DRIVEN ME *MAD!!*

Mary Beaird

http://www.diyhamstercraft.com

Mary Beaird is one of Sweatdrop's two writers. Her current titles are *'Binkan Shounen Kurodzu Kuri'*, in partnership with Sam Brown (a.k.a. Subi), and *'Tetraspace'*, a series of short stories featuring different artists. Her third comic *'Elephant Elephant Hippo Rhino…?'* is her only solo effort. Her featured story is *'Angel's Game: Other Wings'*, with art by Jacqueline Kwong and help from Ken Hoang (a.k.a. Cin), for which many thanks.

I CANNOT SAY. IT WILL BE FINISHED WHEN IT IS FINISHED.

Thank you for reading!

We're all proud to be part of this anthology, and hope you enjoyed reading it. If you liked what you read here, you can find more work by these artists at

www.sweatdrop.com

SEE THE STORY FROM A NEW PERSPECTIVE!

*There are always **two sides** to every story, but it's not often you get to experience **both!***

"Blue is for boys" re-tells the tales from "Pink is for girls" but with a very different emphasis.

See the same characters from a completely new perspective, or even read stories that take place simultaneously alongside one you've already read. Protagonists become antagonists, antagonists become love interests, and some characters transform into something else entirely.

Sweatdrop Studios presents a unique experiment in comic form, intertwining yet also defining male and female sensibilities in manga.

sweatdrop studios

A KICK-ASS SWEATDROP ANTHOLOGY FOR GUYS

BLUE IS FOR BOYS

WITH ARTWORK BY:
- HAYDEN SCOTT-BARON
- VANESSA WELLS
- STEPHANIE DREWETT
- HANNAH SAUNDERS
- SELINA DEAN
- SAM BROWN
- LAURA WATTON
- SARAH BURGESS
- RIK NICOL

ADDITIONAL WRITING BY:
- MARY BEAIRD
- FEHED SAID
- SONIA LEONG

AND FOREWORD BY:
- PAUL GRAVETT

A 'SHONEN MANGA' APPROACH TO NINE SHORT STORIES

PINK IS FOR GIRLS

BLUE IS FOR BOYS

AVAILABLE NOW FROM SWEATDROP STUDIOS!

Cold Sweat & Tears

A Sweatdrop Anthology about Human Emotion. This book compiles ten short stories from previously released collections 'Love, Sweat & Tears' and 'Cold Sweat', along with bonus artwork and information, in perfect bound format. Ten gripping tales that tread the line between love and fear.

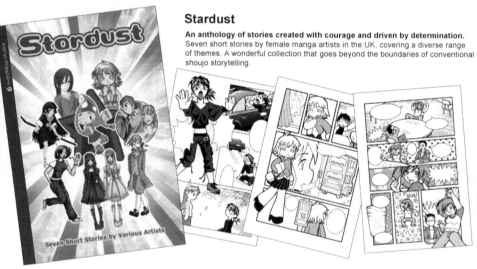

Stardust

An anthology of stories created with courage and driven by determination. Seven short stories by female manga artists in the UK, covering a diverse range of themes. A wonderful collection that goes beyond the boundaries of conventional shoujo storytelling.

Sugardrops

More than a dozen short stories on the theme of 'Cute' ... From the sweet and saccharine to the bizarre and fantastical, every facet of cuteness in manga is explored and unfolded in this themed anthology. With plenty of interesting stories for readers of all ages, this is an ideal introduction to the variety of work within Sweatdrop Studios.

Fantastic Cat volume 1, by Selina Dean

Flying cats and people who fall from the sky!
Oskar loses his memory, but gains some friends. It's a shame they're just a little strange... No matter how far you run (or should that be fly?) your past will always catch up to you.

Looking for the Sun volume 1 & 2, by Morag Lewis

Kite is looking for the sun. Why? Because it's lost...
Somewhere among the myriad worlds there is one which has lost its sun. All the hydrogen's still there at the centre of the solar system, where the sun used to be, but the world is in darkness and will eventually die if something is not done.

Revolution Baby volume 1, by Sam Brown (Subi)

ANIME FANS RULE THE COUNTRY ... but it's not the perfect world we imagined
In the midst of the chaos of counterrevolution, idol singer meets bunny girl and they plunge into a maelstrom of music, cliché, students, violent cops, tight bodysuits, great big f--k-off robots, lightspeed martial arts and panties. ONLY A DEUS EX MACHINA ENDING CAN SAVE THEM NOW!

catalogue

available now, from

sweatdrop
ORIGINAL UK MANGA STUDIOS

www.sweatdrop.com